Celebrity Influencers

EMMA WATSON

MARY HERTZ SCARBROUGH

Rourke Educational Media
A Division of Carson Dellosa Education
rourkeeducationalmedia.com

ROURKE'S **SCHOOL to HOME** CONNECTIONS

BEFORE AND DURING READING ACTIVITIES

Before Reading: *Building Background Knowledge and Vocabulary*

Building background knowledge can help children process new information and build upon what they already know. Before reading a book, it is important to tap into what children already know about the topic. This will help them develop their vocabulary and increase their reading comprehension.

Think about it...

1. Why do people enjoy paying attention to celebrities?
2. What is this celebrity famous for?
3. What are some of the qualities about celebrities that make them stand out?
4. What are the similarities and differences between a celebrity and a hero/heroine?
5. How does a person's professional career connect them to personal experiences?
6. How does what we know about the world shape the way we view ourselves?
7. How do our personal experiences shape our view of others?
8. How does the media shape our view of the world and ourselves?

Vocabulary: *Vocabulary Is Key to Reading Comprehension*

Use the following directions to prompt a conversation about each word.

- Read the vocabulary words.
- What comes to mind when you see each word?
- What do you think each word means?

Vocabulary Words:

- *annulled*
- *empower*
- *environmentally*
- *fair-trade*
- *organic*
- *publicize*

During Reading: *Reading for Meaning and Understanding*

To achieve deep comprehension of a book, children are encouraged to use close reading strategies. During reading, it is important to have children stop and make connections. These connections result in deeper analysis and understanding of a book.

Close Reading a Text

During reading, have children stop and talk about the following:

- Any confusing parts
- Any unknown words
- Text to text, text to self, text to world connections
- The main idea in each chapter or heading

Encourage children to use context clues to determine the meaning of any unknown words. These strategies will help children learn to analyze the text more thoroughly as they read.

When you are finished reading this book, turn to the next-to-last page for **After Reading Questions** and an **Activity**.

Table of Contents

Fashionista for Good

Red-carpet regular Emma Watson wants clothes that do more than just look good. Her clothing should be **environmentally** friendly. And the people who make her clothes should have decent working conditions.

environmentally (en-vye-ruhn-MENT-uh-lee): related to Earth and its living things, bodies of water, and atmosphere

You'd never know by looking at it, but Emma's beautiful dress is made from 49 feet (15 meters) of leftover fabric. She wore it on her Beauty and the Beast *tour in 2017.*

At the Met Gala in 2016, fans adored Emma's eco-conscious gown. It was made from recycled plastic bottles spun into fabric. The outfit was lined with **organic** silk. Even the zippers were made with recycled materials.

organic (or-GAN-ik): made using only natural products and without laboratory-made fertilizers or pesticides

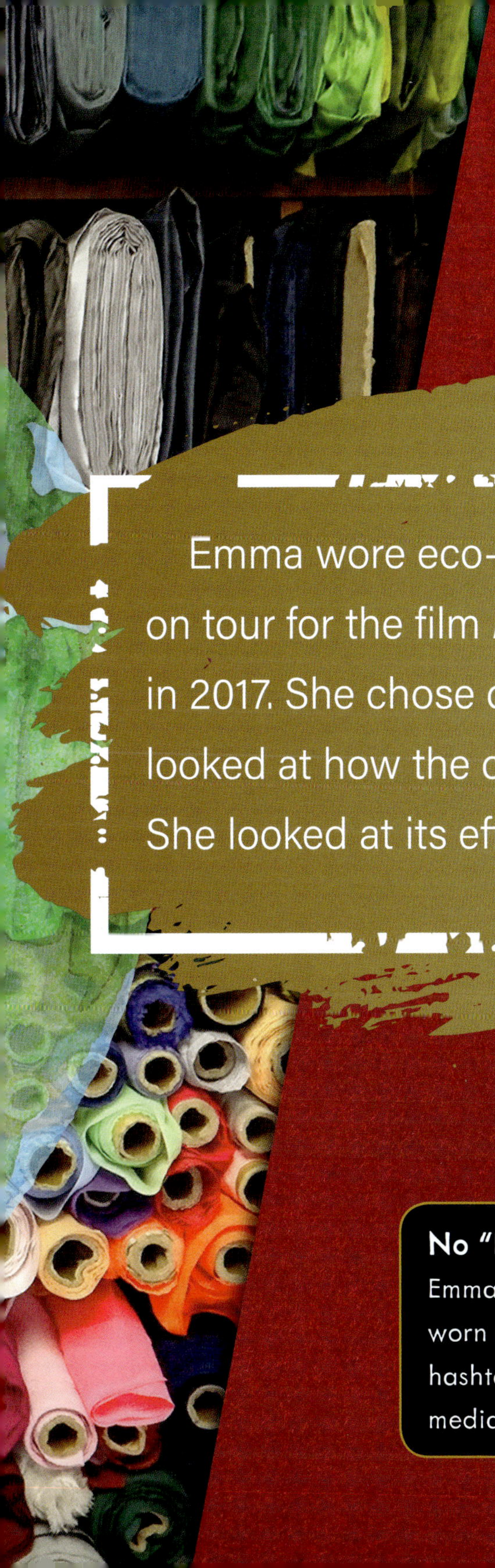

Emma wore eco-friendly fashion while on tour for the film *Beauty and the Beast* in 2017. She chose designers carefully. She looked at how the clothing was produced. She looked at its effect on the environment.

No "Fast Fashion" for Watson

Emma believes clothes should be worn many times. She uses the hashtag #30wears on her social media accounts.

Emma helped design clothing for a **fair-trade** fashion company. She traveled to Bangladesh. She met garment makers and saw their working conditions. She said fair trade "is keeping skills and communities alive."

fair-trade (fair-TRADE): a way of buying and selling products that makes sure the people who make the goods are paid a fair price

Gender Equality Is Everyone's Issue

Emma is a United Nations (UN) Women Goodwill Ambassador. Her role is to help **empower** young women. She leads a campaign to promote gender equality called HeForShe. HeForShe calls for men to help solve equality issues.

empower (em-POU-ur): to help people control their own lives and claim their rights

Noticing Inequality
People called Emma bossy when she was a child. She realized that boys who acted like she did weren't called that.

"Feminism by definition is the belief that men and women should have equal rights and opportunities," Emma said in a UN speech. Nobel Peace Prize winner Malala Yousafzai began calling herself a feminist after hearing Emma's speech.

Malala Yousafzai

Just a Word

"Feminism is another word for equality," Malala said. Before Emma's speech, she felt uncomfortable with the word.

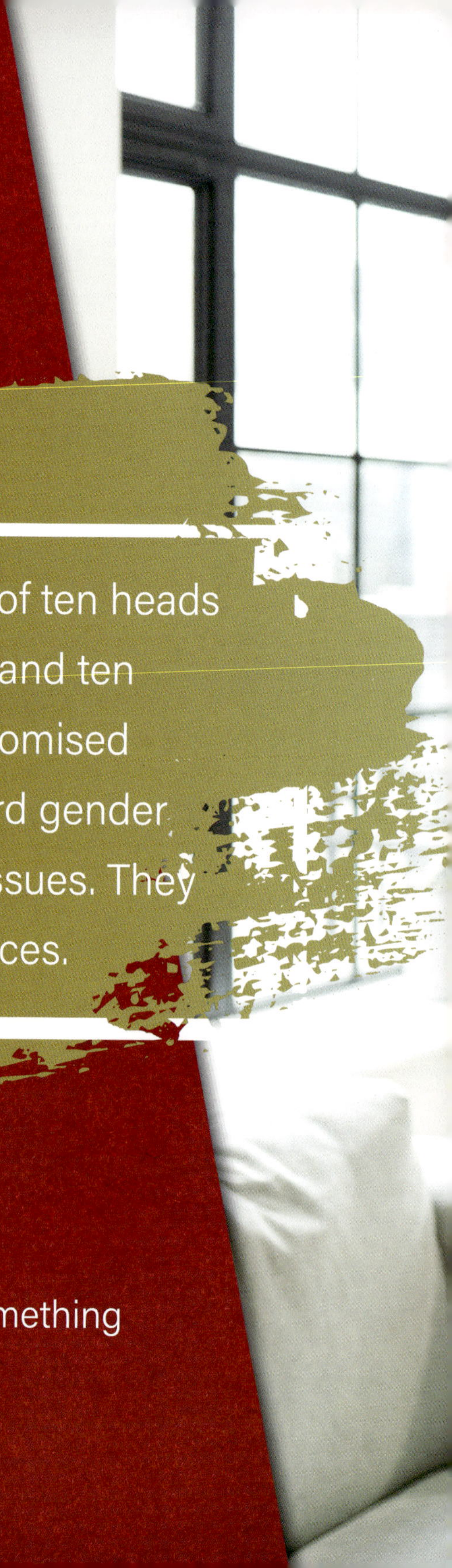

Emma has enlisted the help of ten heads of state, ten corporate leaders, and ten educators. These 30 leaders promised to take measurable steps toward gender equality. They help **publicize** issues. They help change their own workplaces.

publicize (PUHB-li-size): to make something known to as many people as possible

Duty Calls

Emma sometimes gets criticized for working toward gender equality. Emma's response is, "If not me, who? If not now, when?"

Emma was a featured speaker at the One Young World Summit in 2016. This conference brought together 1,300 young adults. Participants came from 196 countries. They discussed problems such as gender equality, the environment, and discrimination.

YOUNG WORLD
one
ORDEM E PROGRESSO
PERU

#METOO
#TIMESUP
WARNING
patagonia

Emma supports the #MeToo movement. In 2018, she donated 1.4 million dollars to the Justice and Equality Fund. The organization fights harassment and discrimination at work.

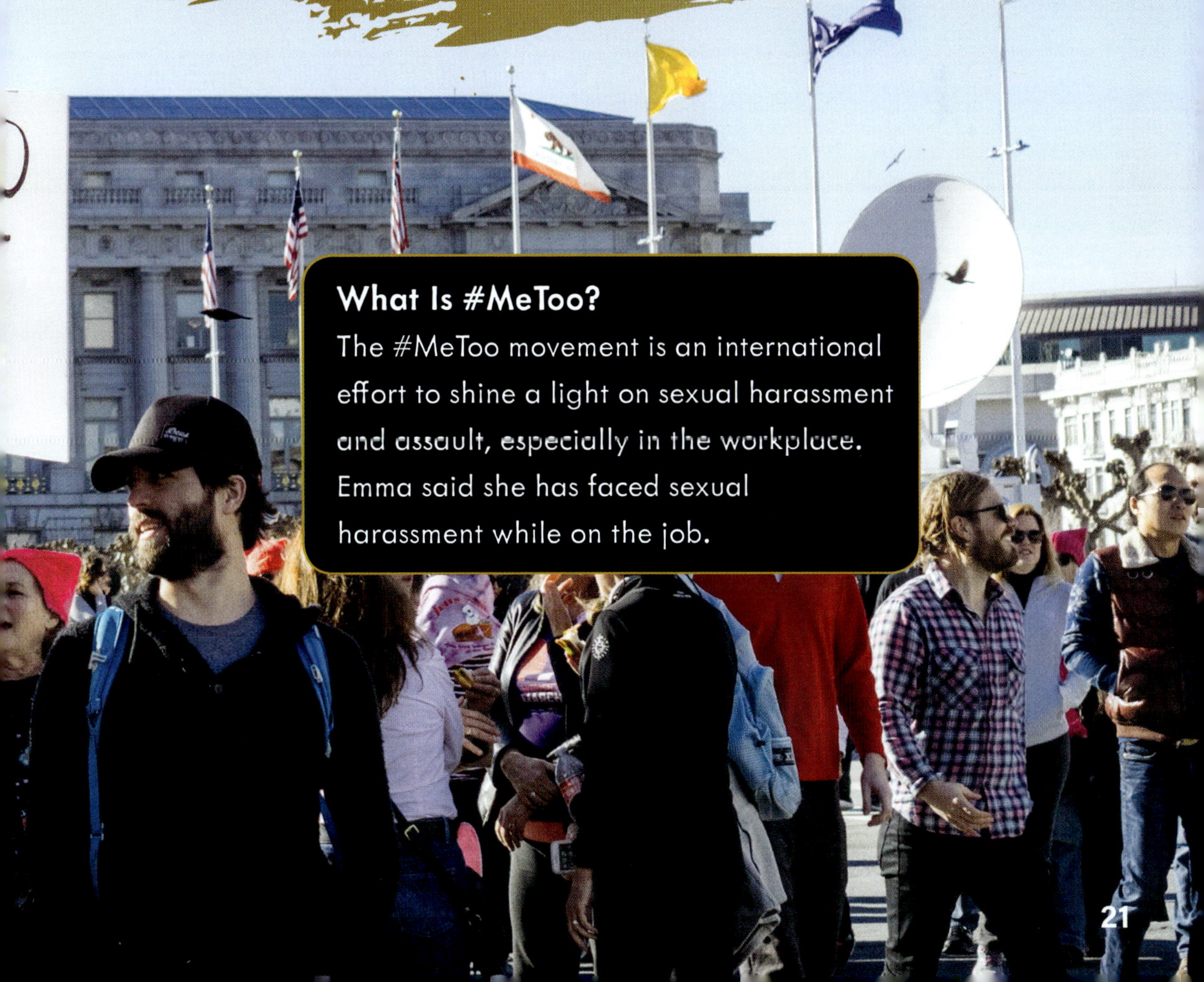

What Is #MeToo?

The #MeToo movement is an international effort to shine a light on sexual harassment and assault, especially in the workplace. Emma said she has faced sexual harassment while on the job.

Efforts to End Child Marriage and Promote Women's Education

Emma hates that teenage girls are sometimes forced into marriage. These girls are often poor. They frequently drop out of school. Many have health problems.

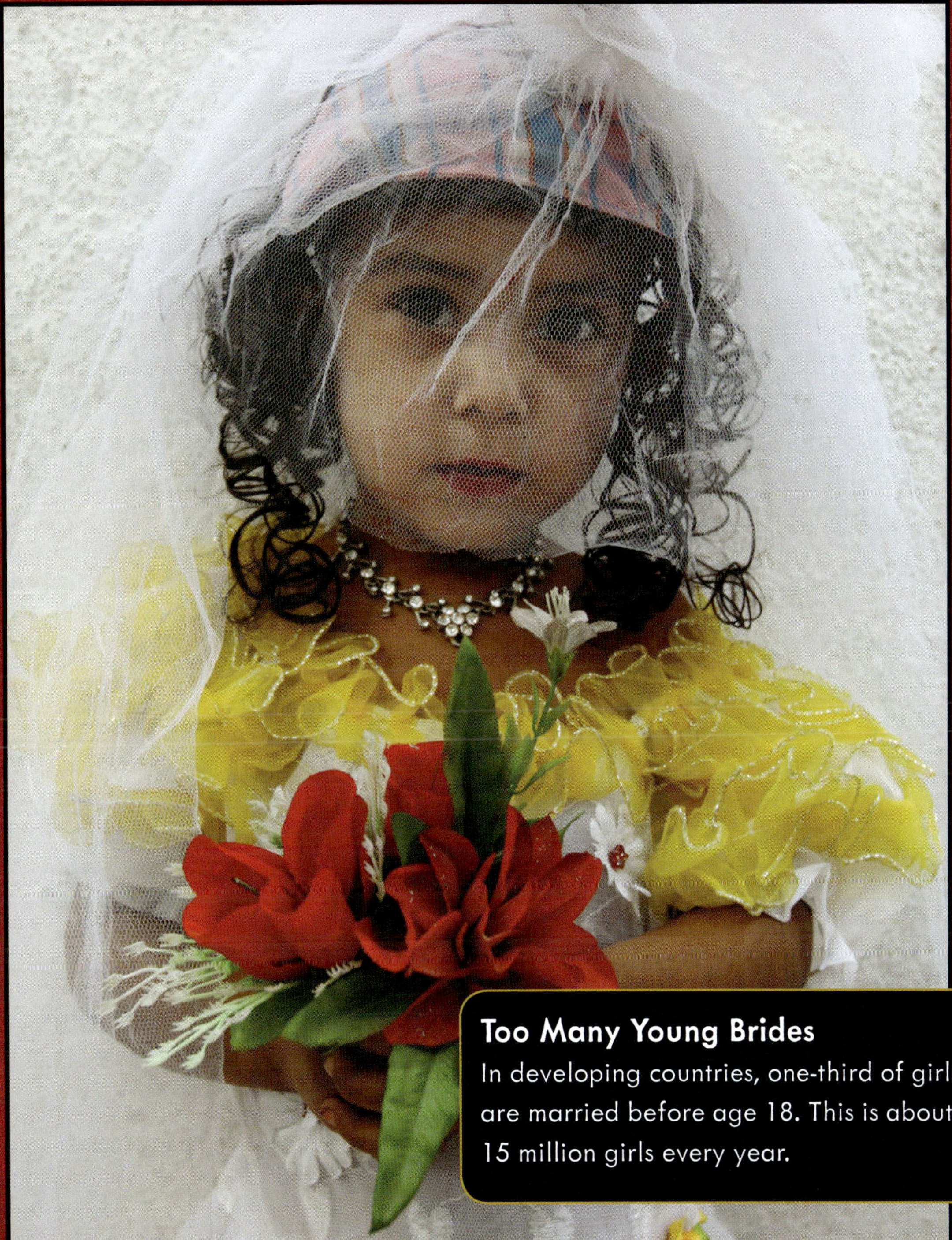

Too Many Young Brides

In developing countries, one-third of girls are married before age 18. This is about 15 million girls every year.

This three-year-old's father engaged her to her seven-year-old cousin. The families agreed that the two will marry when the girl is 14 or 15.

Emma went to Malawi. She met with teen girls and country leaders. She talked about a new law that says girls must be 18 to marry. Some girls were able to have their marriages **annulled**.

annulled (uh-NUHLD): canceled

It Takes a Village

One Malawi chief annulled nearly 1,500 marriages. Chiefs, mothers, and religious leaders supported her. Many girls went back to school.

Zambia has a high rate of child marriage. Many girls drop out of school. Emma visited and bought bicycles. The bikes help women and girls get to school so they don't have to drop out.

Emma started an online feminist book club. It's called Our Shared Shelf. She is known to hide books in different cities. She hopes people will share the books after reading them.

Book Fairies

Our Shared Shelf partnered with a group called The Book Fairies. They have hidden books in more than 100 countries.

Memory Game

Look at the pictures. What do you remember reading on the pages where each image appeared?

Index

After Reading Questions

1. How did this famous celebrity show good citizenship and contribute to the lives of people around the world?
2. What makes this person creative, inventive and notable?
3. Did you learn anything about Emma Watson that surprised you?
4. How do celebrities influence and inspire change?
5. How did the book change your belief about something?

Activity

Imagine that you are a reporter preparing to interview Emma Watson about her charitable causes. Would you want to focus on one of her interests or ask questions about all of them? Why? Jot down your top five questions.

About the Author

Mary Hertz Scarbrough and her family loved reading the *Harry Potter* books together and seeing each movie. Without a doubt, Hermione is her favorite character. As a mom to three daughters, Mary especially appreciates Emma Watson's efforts on behalf of women and girls everywhere.

www.rourkeeducationalmedia.com

PHOTO CREDITS: Cover: ©Press Association via AP images; Page 4: ©Pan Zhiwei / AP images; Page 6: ©Thon_Varirit; page 7: ©Ovidiu Hrubaru / Shutterstock; page 8: ©enviromatic; page 8b: ©saemilee; page 10: ©Liuser; page 13: ©lenant; page 14: ©Simon Davis / DFID; page 14b: ©Wiki; page 15: ©Bebeto Matthews / AP images; page 17: ©visualspace; page 19: ©Dutchmen / Shutterstock; page 20-21: ©Sundry Photography / Shutterstock; page 23: ©Farzana Wahidy; page 24-25: ©Bartosz Hadyniak; page 26-27: ©africa924 / Shutterstock; page 29: ©Sergey Tinyakou

Edited by: Kim Thompson
Cover and interior design by: Rhea Magaro-Wallace

Library of Congress PCN Data

Emma Watson / Mary Hertz Scarbrough
(Celebrity Influencers)
ISBN 978-1-73161-733-0 (hard cover)
ISBN 978-1-73161-269-4 (soft cover)
ISBN 978-1-73161-745-3 (e-Book)
ISBN 978-1-73161-757-6 (ePub)
Library of Congress Control Number: 2019932325

Rourke Educational Media
Printed in the United States of America,
North Mankato, Minnesota